Created by Keith Chapman

First published in Great Britain by HarperCollins Children's Books in 2006

1 3 5 7 9 10 8 6 4 2

ISBN-13: 978-0-00-722313-8
ISBN: 0-00-722313-7

Based on the television series *Fifi and the Flowertots* and the
original script 'Slugsy's Rescue' by Dave Ingham.
© Chapman Entertainment Limited 2006

Printed and bound in China

Slugsy's
Rescue

HarperCollins *Children's Books*

One sunny morning in Flowertot Garden,
there was a very funny noise coming from
Forget-Me-Not Cottage.

BOiiing!   BOiiing!

It was Fifi on her cobweb trampoline.
Bumble and Primrose skipped into the
garden as Fifi bounced on to the ground.

"Hi Bumble. Hi Primrose," Fifi waved.
"I'm supposed to be meeting someone this morning but
I've forgotten who it is..."
Primrose and Bumble looked at each other and laughed.
"Er, us?" giggled Bumble. "Fifi Forget-Me-Not, forgot!"

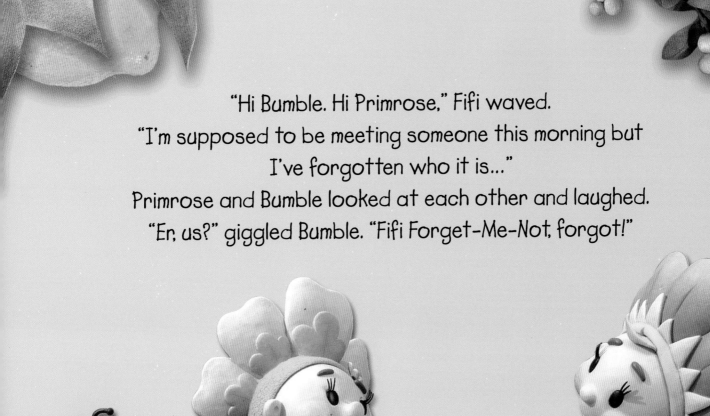

Outside the Apple Tree House, Stingo and Slugsy were peering through the telescope at a particularly delicious looking apple. "Oooh, I can't wait for it to fall!" Slugsy said, licking his lips.

"Fall?" yelped Stingo. "FALL? We can't let it fall!
It will get all bruised and yucky"
"Mmm, bruisssed and yucky,"
sighed Slugsy, "sssounds nice."
"No it doesn't," said Stingo,
disgusted, "which is why you, my
slimy friend, will lower it to the
ground. Don't worry, you'll be
perfectly safe!"
Slugsy frowned at Stingo. He
didn't like the sound of this
plan one little bit.

Back in Fifi's garden,
the Tots were having lots
of fun on the seesaw.
"Hey Bumble," called
Fifi, "do you want
to go really high?"

Slugsy, however, was not sure he wanted to go really high at all! Nervously, he sat strapped into a harness at the bottom of the Apple Tree House. "I am a brave ssslug," he whispered to himself, "I am a brave ssslug."

Up at the top of the tree, Stingo had tied the end of the rope from the harness to the apple... "Ready, Slugsy?" he yelled, letting go of the rope and jumping on the apple to free it.

Whoosh!

Slugsy flew high up into the air and the apple dropped down on the ground. But Slugsy didn't follow the apple down. He was stuck in mid-air!

"What do you think you are doing up there?" yelled Stingo angrily. "You were supposed to lower the apple GENTLY to the ground!"

"I tried, honessst I did, but it was jusssst too heavy!" cried Slugsy. "Can you get me down, bosss?"

"Rotten Raspberries!" grumbled Stingo, buzzing off to find help. "Use your walkie talkie to keep in touch and whatever you do, DON'T LOOK DOWN!"

"I am a brave ssslug," whimpered Slugsy. "I am a brave ssslug..."

"Stingo to Slugsy,
are you OK? Over,"
Stingo muttered
into his walkie talkie
as he arrived at
Webby's web, where
the friendly spider
was asleep.

"Noooo! Helllp!" yelled Slugsy.
"Did someone say they needed help?"
said Webby, waking suddenly.
"Erm, yes," smiled Stingo sweetly.
"It's Slugsy, he's, well, stuck up a tree."

In Fifi's garden, the Tots were having great fun. They were taking it in turns to jump from the trampoline onto the seesaw to make Bumble fly high into the air. Now they were having a well earned rest.

"Er, hello," waved Stingo. "Having fun?"
"What do you want?" asked Primrose suspiciously.
"Me? Nothing! It's Slugsy, he's, er, stuck up a tree..." said Stingo.

"Then there's no time to lose!" Fifi said,
dusting down her dungarees. "Pip, Primrose
and Stingo, you take the trampoline. We have
a slug to rescue and I've got an idea!"
Soon Stingo and the Tots were back by the
Apple Tree House with their playthings.

As he reached Slugsy, Bumble grabbed hold of the rope and together, they slowly began to lower to the ground.

"You can open your eyes now, Slugsy," laughed Fifi as they landed gently.

Slugsy looked around in amazement. "Oh, thank you!
THANK YOU!" he yelped, giving Bumble a big bear hug.
"Well, if it wasn't for my quick thinking," said Stingo
buzzing over. But just as he stepped in the empty
harness, Slugsy let go of the rope... "You'd still be up

THEEEERRE!"

Stingo flew high into the apple tree!
"Look at him go!" laughed Pip as the
juicy apple hit the floor with a thud for
the second time.

"I thought
you wanted
to bring the apple down
gently, bosss?" Slugsy said
into his walkie talkie.
"Oww! Rotten
Raspberries! Over."
Stingo replied.

"All this excitement has made me thirsty!" said Pip,
once Stingo was safely on the ground.
"Me too," agreed Fifi, looking over at the juicy
apple. "Mmm, delicious apple juice."
"Leave it alone!" yelled Stingo, buzzing
in front of the apple. "It's mine!"
"Actually," said Slugsy, "half the apple
belongsss to me and as you all helped
sssave me, you can all ssshare it!"

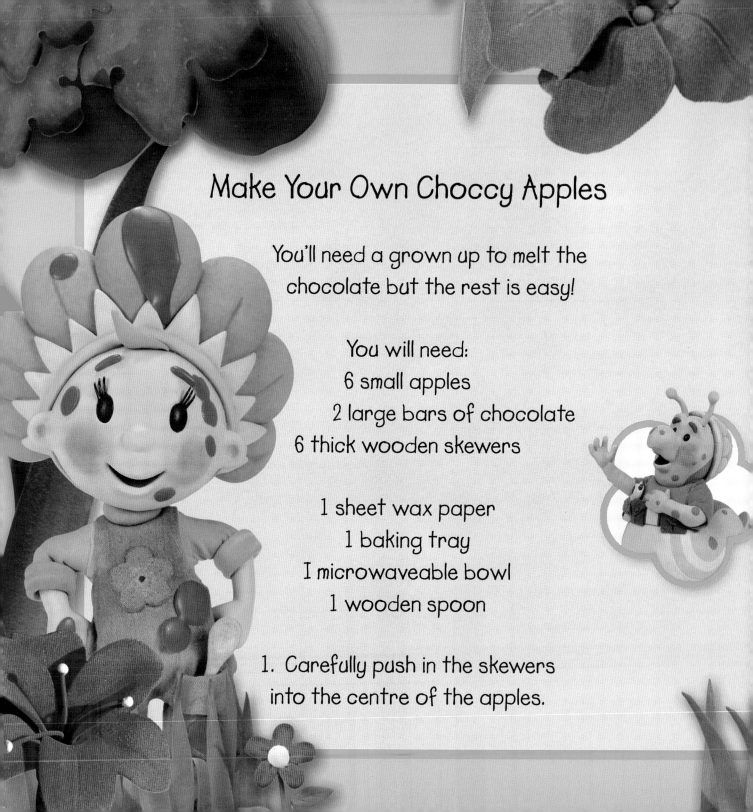

Make Your Own Choccy Apples

You'll need a grown up to melt the
chocolate but the rest is easy!

You will need:
6 small apples
2 large bars of chocolate
6 thick wooden skewers

1 sheet wax paper
1 baking tray
I microwaveable bowl
1 wooden spoon

1. Carefully push in the skewers
into the centre of the apples.

2. Break up chocolate and pop all the pieces into a microwaveable bowl. Ask a grown-up to melt the chocolate in the microwave.

3. Once all the chocolate is melted, let it cool for a minute or so before carefully dipping in the apples on their skewers.

4. Pop all the chocolate-coated apples onto the wax paper lined baking tray and leave them to set in the fridge.

5. In one hour, check the chocolate has set – yummy!

Talking Fifi Forget-Me-Not

Talk 'n' Sneeze Bumble

Push 'n' Go Mo

Forget-Me-Not Cottage Playset

Fifi and the Flowertots is a magazine aimed at 3-5 year olds who love to be busy, just like Fifi. Join the Flowertot fun in Fifi's world!

Have even more Flowertot fun with these Fifi story and activity books!

Chocolate Surprise is out on DVD now!

Visit Fifi at www.fifiandtheflowertots.com